Victoria
and the
Crowded
Pocket

Carolyn Sloan & Mary Murphy

PUFFIN BOOKS

To Peter, Katie and all the Kellys ~ MM

PUFFIN BOOKS

Published by the Penguin Group
Penguin Books Ltd, 80 Strand, London WC2R ORL, England
Penguin Putnam Inc., 375 Hudson Street, New York, New York 10014, USA
Penguin Books Australia Ltd, 250 Camberwell Road, Camberwell, Victoria 3124, Australia
Penguin Books Canada Ltd, 10 Alcorn Avenue, Toronto, Ontario, Canada M4V 3B2
Penguin Books India (P) Ltd, 11 Community Centre, Panchsheel Park, New Delhi – 110 017, India
Penguin Books (NZ) Ltd, Cnr Rosedale and Airborne Roads, Albany, Auckland, New Zealand
Penguin Books (South Africa) (Pty) Ltd, 24 Sturdee Avenue, Rosebank 2196, South Africa

Penguin Books Ltd, Registered Offices: 80 Strand, London WC2R ORL, England

www.penguin.com

First published by Kestrel 1973
This edition published by Viking 2001
Published in Puffin Books 2002
1 3 5 7 9 10 8 6 4 2

Text copyright © Carolyn Sloan, 1973
Illustrations copyright © Mary Murphy, 2001
All rights reserved

The moral right of the illustrator has been asserted

Set in phoenix chunky

Made and printed in Italy by Printer Trento Srl

British Library Cataloguing in Publication Data
A CIP catalogue record for this book is available from the British Library

ISBN 0-140-56713-5

When Victoria was a
very small kangaroo,

she lived in her
mother's pocket.

It was not a
STAYING STILL
place, like a house.
It was like living in a ...

flying

jumble

sale.

One day,

when her mother

had bounced

about **TOO** much,

Victoria jumped

out of

the pocket.

Victoria went to Mrs Koala.
"Please let me live the way
your children live," she said.

"STAY ON."

"All right," said the
koala kindly.
"Climb on my back and ..."

Away they went through the trees.

Victoria

fell

off

into

a

puddle

(and was scratched by a tree).

"Thank you, Mrs Koala,"
she gasped. "But it's safer in
my mother's pocket; I will go
back there."

Victoria

hopped

back

to

her

mother,

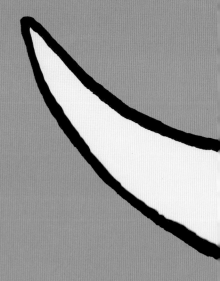

and for a while
she was very happy.

Then her mother found a spiky cactus in a pot and a goldfish in a bowl, and put them in her pocket on top of Victoria.

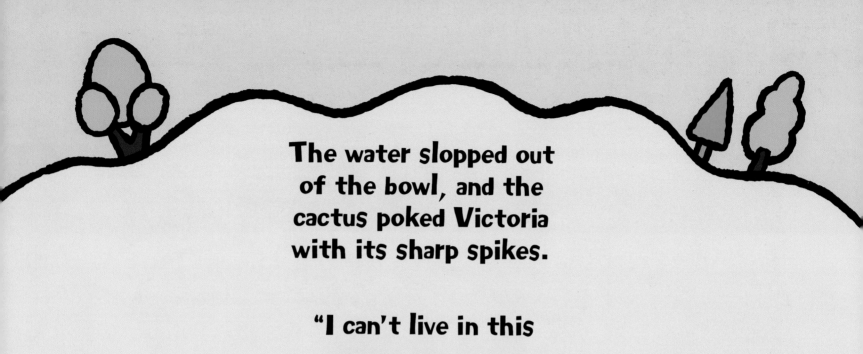

The water slopped out
of the bowl, and the
cactus poked Victoria
with its sharp spikes.

"I can't live in this

MUDDY,

SPIKY

MESS,"

she said, and jumped out.

She went to
Mrs Rabbit and
said, "Please
take me home
with you."

"Please yourself," said the rabbit,
and she started to run very fast.

The little
kangaroo was
running
out of
bounce
when
Mrs Rabbit
suddenly
shot down
a hole.

"You can't live down a

HOLE,"

puffed Victoria.

But Mrs Rabbit did.

The hole was just big enough for her,

but much too small for Victoria.

Mrs Kangaroo spring-cleaned
her pocket, and for a
little while it was
a good place
to be.

But soon she began to find all sorts of
things that she put in her pocket

ON TOP

of Victoria. She found ...

In the end she went
back to her mother.

Victoria told her mother about the places she had tried to live in that would be better than the pocket.

"You are too big for my pocket now," said her mother. "But there is someone else there. LOOK!"

Victoria looked and there was a baby kangaroo so small that it was hardly there at all.

Hello, Victoria.

"That is your brother," said Mrs Kangaroo.

"But where shall I live now?"
said Victoria.

"WITH ME,"

said her mother. "We can all
three go anywhere we like,
and if we don't like it when
we get there we can bounce
somewhere else."

And the three kangaroos
bounced away to a place,
just to see if they liked it.